The Homecoming

Short Stories

Uma Sharma

Ukiyoto Publishing

All global publishing rights are held by

Ukiyoto Publishing

Published in 2025

Content Copyright © Uma Sharma

ISBN 9789370095069

All rights reserved.

No part of this publication may be reproduced, transmitted, or stored in a retrieval system, in any form by any means, electronic, mechanical, photocopying, recording or otherwise, without the prior permission of the publisher.

The moral rights of the author have been asserted.

This is a work of fiction. Names, characters, businesses, places, events, locales, and incidents are either the products of the author's imagination or used in a fictitious manner. Any resemblance to actual persons, living or dead, or actual events is purely coincidental.

This book is sold subject to the condition that it shall not by way of trade or otherwise, be lent, resold, hired out or otherwise circulated, without the publisher's prior consent, in any form of binding or cover other than that in which it is published.

www.ukiyoto.com

To Ananya,
You are the wind beneath my wings

Contents

The Homecoming	1
I am	5
Till Eternity ….	9
Hues	17
Picking the Pieces	21
Unconditional Love	32
About the Author	*40*

The Homecoming

How do I pretend that nothing has happened? I can't! I tried not to think of the grave, dark thoughts but they are my constant companion. Like a loyal pet quietly waiting in the background while I thought they were gone. Well, I can't describe them lurking in the dark; they are docile. Waiting to be acknowledged. Silently waiting for their turn which they deserve as I have created them somewhere in the past. They were born in those moments of anger when I clouded my mind with myopic judgements. I took a few deep breaths and looked outside my window. A round ball of orange sun looked back at me. A silentious breeze passed my face ruffling the strands of hair falling loosely on my face. The queued thoughts started to trickle like children in the park. Its no stopping them I gave in.

Its miraculous how we fall victim to our own misgivings. Denying ourselves the gratification of our own purpose. Aimlessly moving from one doubt to another. It is indescribable how gradually we become worthless in our own eyes. I walk over to the kitchen to take out yesterday's leftovers from the refrigerator to re- heat. Rahul is out of town so no need to cook dinner. I can eat my dinner quietly and fall back in my reverie. Its nice to be alone. The lamp on the side of the sofa gleams its shadow creating patterns on the wall. No matter how much I try to forget about him he finds his way in my thoughts. It's been a year since I last met Soham. His face still lingers in my thoughts. Sometimes I call his name. There are times when I don't feel anything except anger for him. The squeamish hot feeling in my gut. I want to cry but tears seem to elude me like him.

Is love perishable? Can it fade with time? It does seem sometimes that love can't be incurred. The grief of separation is unbearable. How to pick up the pieces of your heart blown away by indifference. The bland state of affairs that do not pique your state of mind. Its either briny or saltless. You move from one state of mood from another inharmoniously. It does feel like a see-saw. The memories that put me on high once now take me to the darkest pit of hell. I have no use of them. They are rusting in some dark corner that I do not want to touch. In the night I try to reach out to some oblivious hand to hold in my dreamless sleep. It comes back untouched like my messages to him. How to understand those endless hours of waiting, frequently checking messages for one reply that never comes. Only a blank screen staring at my face. I want to tell him how I feel. I want him to know how vitriol I feel. How much it hurts.

I woke up in the middle of the night, breathless. I looked around, a mute darkness stared back at me. It was difficult to breathe. I closed my eyes and took some deep breaths to calm myself. It was another dream of his. Another barren dream that has spun its tentacles of unrequited hope around my desires. I dreamed of Soham, my Soham! He felt distant, like the moon in a dark sky; real but out of reach. It felt like I've walked on a journey with him though he has returned. I'm still searching my way back home. Its always fascinating to realize that our recovery is always hidden in our darkest thoughts. The downward spiral is the path to return. This lowest pit of hell showed me the way to heaven. In an instant I realised I'm grieving not because I lost Soham, I'm grieving because I lost myself.

I stepped out in my garden. The yellowish almost dry grass reminded me that I did not water it for a week. The day was bright and sunny. I felt relieved. It is wearisome when you feel a part of yourself is living in a parallel world. This realization woke me up at night. I met my missing part in my dream. A knowing that its arduously on its way to join me. The sadness I felt when I met myself in the dream. That left me breathless. In a heartbreak we don't just grieve losing another we grieve because we lose a part of ourselves too. I realised it was time to meet myself again!

I picked up the water bucket and started spraying water on the grass. The drops of water trickling through the parched soil making it moist somehow soothed my thoughts. The thoughts seem to drift away like clouds on a windy day. My mind was clear and so was my heart. I put the water bucket and pulled the chair which was lying neglected at the edge of the garden. I felt light. There was ease in my movements as if a burden was lifted from my shoulders. An unspoken obligation of my commitment to Soham even when he was not bound with it. Sometimes spoken words hold a silent obligation with which we bind ourselves. I have bound myself to Soham. A part of me kept moving towards him. I looked at a blade of grass drenched with water, it looked greener and more alive as if the water was its long lost part it was searching. I was parched and yellowish and heavy. I was thirsty for my lost part which was shouldering an unsaid obligation that does not exist. I was indifferent towards it. I distant myself in a dark corner trying to forget it while craving for it all this time. Now, I will call it back. It is waiting for me to call it. I remember.

Six months later

I opened my door, it was Rahul, my brother, we have been staying together since my breakup with Soham. The dinner table was ready, I made his favourite pasta. It was time to watch a horror movie. Rahul switched on the TV while I went to get my glasses. I passed the mirror, I stopped to look at my reflection, a smile came on my face. I rise!

I am

In the depths of our heart, we always know love is elusive. It is like sand slipping through the fingers, you can feel but cannot hold it. Seema realized it too. She could feel the salty taste of longing in her dry mouth. This is the third night in a row when she woke up with dry mouth and aching heart. She could hear her heart beating furiously against her chest. It is the same dream all over again. She sat up on bed, took out a cigarette from the packet on the side table and walked out in the balcony. She lit the cigarette and took a deep puff slowly exhaling a long chain of smoke. The distant apartments were slumbering in the night . Every unlit window has its own story to tell. The unsaid dreams locked behind the closed eyelids, draped in sleep. Their occupants head laid restfully on fluffy pillows breaking away from relentless chain of thoughts repeating like merry go round. Like box of matches, the apartments looked animated, except few lit up windows the buildings were somber. A feeling of dark silent night was slowly enveloping Seema. Her mind was quiet.

How comfortable it is to dream! To snuggle under the folds of sleep, oblivious to the weight of mind, to the umpteen thoughts . To be in the world of dreams; a place of liquid boundaries where realities bend to encompass many layers of our being. A very real world at one moment, in another, just a writing in sand. It was the same dream. Seema felt an urge to cry. The dream world respite to many has become a punishment for Seema. For three consequent nights, she saw the same dream. Once again she was in Jatin's arms; comforted and consoled. It felt real and suddenly everything else felt unreal. Is it even real that Jatin has moved out. Seema turned to look at the bed, it laid empty. The bed felt like an icy slab. It seemed as if it laid there; empty, barren since forever. The empty space was heavy as if every breath taken by Jatin is still floating in the air. Seema felt the air to be suddenly heavy. Seema took the last puff of her cigarette and went inside the room.

A slanting sun ray was adorning the centre of the room reflecting the zig zag pattern of the curtains on the floor. Seema opened her eyes it was a breezy morning. She felt the chill in the breeze, she forgot to close her balcony door. Her droopy eyelids were still soaked in sleep. She doesn't remember when she falls back to sleep. It was a dreamless sleep. She looked outside with sleep-soaked eyes, it was almost afternoon. She looked at the alarm clock by the bedside table it showed 11.30 am. Seema rushed to the bathroom. A quick bath relaxed her. She dressed up and head out to meet Jatin for lunch. Although they are separated, they still meet occasionally for lunch or coffee. It is impossible for her to live with him again no matter how much she wants to live with him. His memories feel like old wounds that still hurt from time to time. They compromised to remain friends.

Seema hailed an auto. Though the restaurant was just three blocks away from her house, she didn't feel like walking. It was an autumn afternoon, warm and breezy. The bright sun outside was in stark contrast with Seema's gloomy mood. It is an incorrect metaphor to compare a relationship with seasons. Relationship is like a river flowing under a bridge. The same water never flows back it only flows forward. Today would be yesterday which will only exist in memory like leftover food in a discarded plate. Seema came out of her reverie. Auto came to a halt. She paid the driver then quickly turn towards the door of the restaurant. Her heart jumped at the sight of Jatin. Jatin was sitting at their usual spot, engrossed in his tablet. Seema stood for a minute to compose herself. She slowly reached to the table. Jatin looked up and smiled. They have divorced a year ago.

Seema took her seat across Jatin. They know eachother for almost a decade. Their seven years marriage was going strong when Jatin decided to move out. Seema smiled back at Jatin. A relationship is like a river where each partner finds its own trajectory. Jatin found his path in spirituality. He has become a celibate. He has joined an ashram and left Seema and his job. Sometimes we do not need a third person to break a relationship, sometime the partners outgrow each other. Seema took a sip of her brewed, hot coffee. Jatin wanted to discuss the selling of their apartment which was co-owned by her. It is amazing but heart-breaking to realise that a home built of not just brick and mortar but every moment we have shared together, the struggles we had, a place we call our own has a price to it. It is not forever, like it felt when we built it, its just another temporary contract, just an apartment like many we pass haphazardly, standing without a purpose.

Jatin was talking as a matter of fact way as if its not his home,as if he has never lived in it. Seema took another sip of her coffee. She felt her home was a means to an end for Jatin. Suddenly, she felt a surge of energy like an epiphany. It was indeed a means to an end for him and so was she! A realization dawn to her: everything is a means to an end for Jatin even his spirituality, maybe. It was always about what he could get out of anything and nothing was enough. Does anything really means to him? May be nothing. However, she is enough; her life is enough. She doesn't have to become a means to some end.

Seema got up. Her cup was half full of coffee. She gave a last look to Jatin and turned away. She is free now. Her heart was filled with gratitude for her life, for memories and experience. It is a new day, a new beginning!

Till Eternity ....

It is a wonder how words lack to perorate anything that matters; fragrance of freshly brewed tea in the morning, the colour of the flower, the feeling of being in love. Words are like scattered half eaten fruits on the ground dropped after satiating the hunger of the birds. Words cannot convey the real feeling, they can't! it is their inherent nature. The evasive nature of words make love equivocal in its expression. It can only be explicit through conjecture. Love as elusive as it is, in its uncanny way makes itself known wordlessly. Sweta looked in the mirror. It is to her reflection that she shares her deepest thoughts. His eyes reminds her of the mirror. It is miraculous how he understand her thoughts.

She looked at him. He finally came. It was a long, restless wait. He took his seat quietly. Her heart skipped a beat when their eyes met. He once told her they know each other from many lifetimes. Yes, she saw him in her dreams he was a priest and she was a common village girl. Their path crossed many times in her dreams. There is a fragile contour almost unpalpable exists between dream and reality. The aqueous frame of dreams vanquishes the distance between them. In the dreams, there exist many worlds in which they exist in many forms and names. In her dreams she was the cliff holding him on its edge while carrying him in her arms. She is the great Gaia, her mossy surface holding his feet pulling him to herself, not letting him fall into the abyss of the ocean. She protected him to protect herself.

There existed a time not long ago, when there were no dreams. Sweta felt his gaze on her. It was the time before they met. There was darkness within her. The dreams were hollow, there were no stories to tell. A black hole pulling her within itself, engulfing her in its darkest corner. Every night was the same colourless, dry sleep. Waking up in the morning was a chore. Sweta knew she was saved by his smile. He saved her from herself. Now, it was her turn. He smiled and released a sigh of relief. This is their last meeting as he is moving out of the country for two years. Two years is not long but when every minute becomes a wait, a longing to see him again, two years become an eternity.

Sweta felt relaxed. It is ages since she felt satiated. She lived with unquenchable thirst to belong, to come home to rest. Her life seemed random, un-purposeful like a trajectory of water outflowing aimlessly in mud. In this deluge he found her. It is his presence in her life that gave her a path to walk with purpose. He accepted her wilderness, her solitude. She did not have to pretend to be domesticated by pruning her thoughts and being. Sweta felt a hole in her heart. Is it possible for her to live so far from him. To go on living without his ubiquity in her life. In her dreams he lived with her for thousand years till eternity. A realisation hit her everything around her is changing while she is the same. Would he change too?

It was a small village which she saw in her dream. It was a quaint place with dishevelled trees sprouting in places. He was resting against one of the trees waiting for her. She walked into the meadow . It felt like a long walk to reach him. He had fire in his eyes. He told her he was leaving her and moving to another town. How she wanted to protect him from this world. She wanted to scream his name out loud, when she woke up. Sweta felt that she is still in the dream. For the first time she felt the contour between the dream and reality has become tangible. She felt if she pinches herself, she will realise it is just a dream and nothing has changed.

She woke up from her reverie. He smiled again as if he read her thoughts. He came closer to her and held her hand. The touch of his hand in her made her feel rejuvenated. Sweta felt a hope. Somewhere far a horizon was forming. There is a place in this existence where they meet. It is their horizon! The world came to a standstill. They exist not just in this time and space but in many time and space in millions of universe, simultaneously. Living a hundred lives in that moment. He looked in her eyes. It was a complete moment like a clear blue sky with thousand flowers colouring the earth below. The universe was smiling in their rythmn.

She couldn't speak a word to him. They just looked at each other. As if words cannot express the lifetimes of life living within them. The soul recognises but mind has questions. There is so much left unsaid between them. It seems an eternity is needed to understand. But it is this moment that seems eternal. Isn't eternity a moment. A moment that is complete in existence which gets its meaning in the silence of this meeting. This eternal moment started when their eyes met.

They stood in silence. Their path has crossed again. They will survive another life . This distance has only brought them together. The old dream has ended it is time for new dreams and new adventures. He is the same priest and She was the village girl. How did that dream ended She doesn't know, but she knows how this meeting will end. It is time to renew new friendships. A new though unknown path has emerged. She is ready to walk on it with him.She smiled and ran towards him. He just stood with open arms. In that moment she knew how it ended in her dreams. It never ended. They lived through the eternity.

I didn't think I could tell this in my own words. It just boiled down to the surface from a vagabond thought to unspoken words. All this while, I thought I didn't have much to say. How to express the vacuum of my mind? Compare to the cool breeze of thoughts into words, this was stone cold silence. Just gut wrenching, almost engulfing in its darkness.

Then I found a pen and an old diary; under the books, covered in dust. The old rusty thoughts at the corner of my mind came tumbling down like a stack of book balanced unevenly on a book shelf. The silence was cold, unorganised like dishevelled hair. The tuning of my thought was disarray. I realised this confusion when thoughts swirl but could not realise their existence in words. In the by lane of memory she still exists. In my memory, she doesn't sit on a pedestal with golden wings and shiny tiara. She lives just like she lived any ordinary day. If she would have sat on a pedestal, I would have revered her and left that moment as it is and moved on, but how can I ever forget her mundaneness. The simplicity with which she talks, her tone of voice, her simple jokes, the look of her tired eyes after a long day at office. The greatness can be forgotten it is simplicity that penetrates into the pores of our skin.

It was years ago but the memory of our first meeting is still vivid. I met Sangeeta in a coffee shop across my apartment. It was dusk, the sky was mellifluent orange. A light breeze grazed my face as I entered the coffee shop. As if the universe was hinting of what was to come. I walked towards the counter to place my order when I heard a meek voice called asking for my attention. I turned around and there she was, eloquent, effusive, looking straight at me. If we could collect all the moments and keep them store to relive again, this was the moment I wanted to relive again and again. I can live this moment till eternity. May be that was eternity that existed from eons of time. In that moment our past, present and future became one.

It became a routine for us to meet at the coffee shop. Sangeeta has moved to an apartment two blocks from the coffee shop. She was a buddying writer with tremendous potential. She passed away a year ago. Sometimes it feels she never existed and sometimes it seems she never ceased to exist. Death is an inevitable illusion. It makes life quantifiable. From death existence becomes a make believe. The memory becomes a reality because it is the only place the departed exists. Sangeeta's memories are like fragrance of roses, they linger on. The inevitability of death is our greatest fear. The thought of complete annihilation can scare anyone who believed life is permanent. However, one thing that even death cannot annihilate is the memory of the beloved. But what about us who are tormented by the memory of our beloved. Is it really a solace ? to whom? Maybe the dead feel compensated from the ultimate betrayal of life. To us who are left behind our life becomes disparate.

Every day, I walk on the same path which I and Sangeeta have tread a year ago. The flowers on the trees on the sidewalk still exuberate the same fragrance. The same seasons come and go at the same time. Everything is same, everyone is same. However, I feel undone! While in the moment we forget to live. We contemplate about future and believe this moment will continue forever. Meanwhile forgetting that a moment exists here and now and we'll never find another one like it. I took a sip of my coffee and looked outside. My bearings were heavy. Sometimes, it is a herculean task to move out of my apartment and come to the coffee shop. This walk to the coffee shop is the assurance that I give to my perfunctory life. The moment has long past but I reminisce. This relentless torture is the only way I prove my fidelity to her. Remembering her is like a ritual I have to follow zealously.

I took the last sip of my coffee and decided to walk back to my apartment. Is their any respite for me? Do I have to live this desolate life till the end? Like an answer to my prayers, a leaf fell from the tree. It is natural for seasons to change. So, is life! This dried leaf was once a sprout, fresh, alive, breathing. The dried leaf is yet to meet its destiny. It is its amalgamation to the soil is when it will arrive to its destiny. The soil that helped it to grow is its destiny. The creation and the destruction happen in one and the same place. Sangeeta did not leave me she still exists in me. The part in me that loved her is still with her. It's the soil that will nourish her in the journey to meet her. Her part which loved me is with me. It is nourishing me in my journey to meet my destiny. My love is not unreturned. It exists in everything around me.

Sangeeta exists in every core. I found her in the fragrance of the brewing tea, in the slight nip of the morning. In the bloom of the flower, I reckon her. I found her in depths of my heart. Death is inevitable but so is life. It cannot snatch the countless minutes I spent with her. They are alive in my essence . I have become a part of her and she is alive in me. Death could not win. In some quirky way im still alive in her.

In the thousands particle of smoke that evaporated in the sky, I exist in all of them. It will be till eternity.

Hues

The Sun setting in the horizon left a trail of orange hue in the sky. The dusk sprayed in pink stood mutely, before the day dissolves into the depths of the night. I stood by the window, a silent spectator witnessing the explosion of colours in the sky. It amazes me to realize how can an empty space becomes apparently colourful like a vicarious life. An unnamed, undefined commotion surges leaving a dull pain in my gut. I am in a six-by-six dark square box scratching the wall with my nails to let the light in. Breathing in and out desperately while gasping for air. A part of me is torn, its vestige is still etched somewhere in my memories. The gnawing realisation of your absence, a blank space left by you as if an abyss will engulf my existence. I stitched up the scattered parts of me leaving the spaces for the missing parts. The fragments lost call to me like a wolf howling for its mate. I lost them in stolen moments of our togetherness. They are waiting in the last sip of coffee that was left in the cup which you made for me last time. They are left in the ruffle of the bedsheet when we made love. They are soaked in the pillow on which I cried on the morning you left. They are scattered in the endless memories of you which now prick my skin like polyester.

The Homecoming

It is four months and two days since Rajiv left. It is impossible to measure time when the time has reversed. In my mind Im reliving the past with every memory scrutinised, to find the answer for the present. A look in the eye or a wary smile, something that may hint of the present without him. A flaw that Ive missed which will make his absence bearable. My feelings for him are an undeniable fact about me. In loving Rajiv Ive found myself as it happened after losing him, I lost a part of me. Is love the answer to all the pain?

The life I've known is lying like dust on the window sill. I scratch the wall of your silence with my broken nails to find a place to become myself again. This unbelonging leaves me incoherent of my own existence. Is there a purpose to be alive? An animated life! I'm playing an old drum beat on repeat. It never stops, it never ends! Thoughts move fast in a shuffle. Randomly appearing in a continuous loop. A longing appears like a slow buzzing of bees somewhere far, a long-forgotten story starts to weave itself in my mind. Is it hope or a call? like the changing colors of the evening sky. The hope of a new day beckons me to rise. An old memory recollects: a rose drenched in dew, and air mingled with its fragrance. A puff of an old memory nudged me to look behind, the door was always there while I scratched the walls. The torn leaves have dried up while the new, sprouts away. The longing has subsided as a new day starts.

A deep awareness of the present moment grew making me realize my own existence apart from you. I exist! I can exist without you. It is believable to lose and find yourself again. The thought slowed; my breath relaxed. It is possible to live one moment at a time without escaping in the past. It is possible to savour my life one bite at a time. To feel the air without being burdened with memories. To own my life and not as borrowed from you. To be relieved from the pain of being undone. To become whole in each breath. I live on! The struggle to remain extant in the abyss is relentless. Life in all its truth sustains withstanding the loss and struggles. It fights for its survival like a fish pulled out of water. It writhers and strive to remain whole. This is the nature of life. The life existing in me shimmy to find its way back to its dwelling.

I introspect the futility of the time passed. Doesn't love a precious part of life then why do I feel it ruined all. Doesn't it is an answer to all questions? Then why I feel Im diverted from my purpose. Im left empty without directions. May be its due to I forgot to love myself. My love for Rajiv was consuming me so much so that I forgot about my dreams and aspirations. May be it was not love but way to feel belong, not an outcast, ignored almost forgotten. Indeed, love is engrossing. In the desperation to belong we hide ourselves, almost forget who we are. The desire to prove our love we ignore the call of our soul.

It is time to find myself again. To search for that part of myself that knows the truth in its raw form. That part of me that knows Im enough and do not need to underline my self by someone else. I decide to release myself from bondage of approvals of others. My wings are clipped by me. To tied my freedom to someone else It is time to redeem my soul, to dust off the fears and insecurities. It is time to live in the present moment. To put past back where it belongs and let it be.

The freedom to live as I choose to live is my choice. I released a deep breath. The dusk disappeared in the night. Some where high in the sky a star twinkled as if the night smiled with me . It is soothing to look at the embalming darkness. I turned to look at the room, it was silent as if listening to my breath. I went to switch on the lamp and my phone rang, Rajiv's name was staring back at me. I pressed ignore and left the phone at the side table.

Picking the Pieces

Happiness is inevitable, life becomes a relentless pursuit of happiness. Even if the last bone breaks, we still expect to gather happiness through the cracks. Shalini released a sigh of relief. The hall is jam packed. It is one year since her book, my life, my story released. The book is a best seller and today is her book's success party organised by her publisher. The first four rows are filled with journalists. Shalini calmed her excitement and walked up to the stage. She looked graceful draped in a white and red sari. Despite being an introvert, she is a very successful marketeer. Her tall and elegant persona, quietly moves towards the stage.

A protracted, rectangle table was placed at the centre of the stage with plush white chairs facing the audience. She chose the centre seat for herself. Shalini always like to choose the centre seat, even in a restaurant she always picked the centre seating. To her, being in the centre felt like companionship with space surrounding her. As if, she is loved and cared for. As a child she always sat between her parents. She felt their warmth around her. An all-encompassing feeling of being protected. After they passed away, she could not feel that protection from anyone except Kavita. In her discussions with Dr Sonali, her therapist, she always shared this lack of warmth in her life.

The Homecoming

Shalini heard a meek hello, she wakes up from her reverie. It was her publisher, Anand. He seated himself next to her. Anand announced to the audience that they are ready to take the questions. Somebody from the media asked, "Are Shalini and Rohit one soul two bodies?" Shalini felt a shiver pass through her spine.

Rohit, how can she forget Rohit. They are one.

Three years ago

Shalini was heading the mktg dept in an MNC. Today, is a successful day, she pitched their company's new product line to the client. She is ecstatic. She is eager to reach home. She has to tell this to Rohit, her Rohit. She wanted to tell Rohit immediately but he doesn't use phone. Shalini's pressed the gas peddle to the ground, she wanted to reach home as fast as possible. She thought of calling Kavita but she realised that Rohit must be waiting for her. They are married for two years. Their marriage is still a secret, Shalini didn't tell her friends about Rohit. After her parents death, she felt safe again when Rohit came into her life.

Her Rohit is different from men whom she dated in the past. He is a philosopher almost a saint. He is a writer and working on his debut book since one year. His ideas are revolutionary. He says that our mind has limitless power, if we understand our mind we can understand the mysteries of this universe. He doesn't like to go out and like to stay at home. Shalini has also stopped going out. She goes to work and come back home to her Rohit.

Since Rohit entered in her life, she has stopped meeting Kavita. Shalini shared a special relationship with Kavita. There was a time when Shalini could not spend a day without meeting Kavita. They talked about their lives, goals and future. They even shared their dreams. It was Kavita who was by her side when she lost her parents. Since the time Rohit came into her life Kavita has vanished from her life. Now, they hardly meet. They even do not talk on the phone.

How much she misses Kavita in her life. When she is in the room the whole space lits up. To Shalini, Kavita is the reason she smiles. Her one liners are hilarious. Kavita can always make her laugh even if she is extremely sad. She misses Kavita. She wants to spend time with Kavita but she could not leave Rohit behind. She cannot understand why she can't they live life like normal people live.

Shalini parked the car in the parking and rush to home. She unlocks the door and goes straight to the study room. Rohit is not there; she checks the bedroom and could not find him. She is dumbfounded, this has never happened. Rohit is always at home to welcome her when she returns from office. She could not understand the reason. It's true they had an argument two days ago.

In the past six months Rohit seem to have changed. He has become moody and uncommunicative. Whenever he talks to Shalini he seems so far away. He talks about exploring the world. Trying a new adventure. He talks about living alone in a quiet place away from the crowd. Shalini is not able to understand Rohit. Two days ago, Rohit suddenly told Shalini he is leaving for a long vacation. When Shalini asked him where is he going, he did not respond. Shalini felt her whole world tumbling down. She begged Rohit to stay and not leave her alone. After pleading for hours Rohit decided to stay. Since then, he is gloomy and does not respond to her. She discussed this with her therapist. Off late, she and Rohit are having arguments frequently. He seems to get disturbed when she asks him to go out on dinner with her. He gets especially disturbed when she asks him to invite his friends. She finds it difficult to understand why he does not like to meet with her friends to. How long can she hide from people about him?

Shalini reached for the bathroom door and opened the bathroom door, Rohit is standing in front of her. She feels relieved.

"I was looking for you everywhere, I thought you went away", she said smiling.

Rohit was silent. He looked at her and said, " where can I go, you never let me." Shalini looked at him with a grave face and replied, " you know Rohit, I can't live without you." Rohit doesn't reply. A smile appeared on his lips. " it's your mind who thinks that you can't live without me. If you look within, you'll find the only person you can't live without is yourself. The only person you love is yourself. You are free but I'm not free. I'm confound to your fear of loneliness. I'm chained by your attachment to your own sense of worth. Your feeling of abandonment has forced to imprison me in your life. Sometimes, I feel I'm not even real, I'm a figment of your imagination, trapped in your memory. " Shalini is aghast. She didn't realise how angry Rohit is with her. She is surprised that how Rohit's accusations are similar to what her therapist thinks her trouble is.

She has been consulting Dr Sonali since two years. Two years ago she suddenly lost motivation in her life. She would get upset very easily and could not calm herself. She could not sleep or eat. On Kavita's suggestion she met Dr Sonali. Kavita thought she may be suffering from depression as her parents died recently in a car accident. It was during this time that Rohit came into her life. Initially, Shalini did not disclose about Rohit to Dr Sonali. After a year, she started discussing Rohit with Dr Sonali too. She wanted Rohit to meet Dr Sonali but he never agreed to accompany her. Shalini discussed her deep attachment to Rohit with her therapist. Dr Sonali suggested that Shalini has to find an inner connection with herself. She thinks Shalini is projecting her need for validation and fear of intimacy on Rohit. Shalini wanted to discuss with Rohit about it. She knows he has answer to all her questions.

She and Rohit use to discuss everything. She was amazed by Rohit's ability to understand her innermost thoughts. His thoughts on life and how living with him motivated her. But, gradually Shalini started having longer discussion with Dr Sonali. Rohit has become distant and a bit aloof. Sometimes, he would not talk for days. He would just sit in the study and stare. This disturbed her and she wants him to consult Dr Sonali.

Dr Sonali has suggested that Shalini should find out more about Rohit's past and his friends. He told her he worked with a publishing company. On Dr Sonali's advice she visited the publisher. But to her surprise she could not find any record which confirmed Rohit ever worked there. Rohit told her that his parents lived in Mumbai. However, he never introduced her to them. Rohit shared to her about his special friend. Shalini felt insecure; may be he wants to go back to her.

Shalini has become more apprehensive about Rohit. Rohit has been hinting her often that he wants to leave her. They again had an argument yesterday. One of his statements was that he is not separate from her but is part of her. Today, she will ask him what did he mean. Shalini unlocked the door. Rohit was in the study. She removed her purse and went straight to him. "Why did you say yesterday that you are part of me?" Shalini questioned. " Yes, I am part of you. A small part in you that loves and wants to belong", replied Rohit not looking at Shalini. "Look at me. What is wrong with us. Why can't we be the way we were?" She asked frustrated. " Because I want to exist too, I want to explore too. I can't remain here, tied to this house, to you", replied Rohit exasperated. " You can live with me and can still explore the world. You don't have to leave me to feel alive", replied Shalini in tears. " I can't exist like this", replied Rohit and left the room. Shalini broke down in tears. She could not understand him. She is feeling demotivated and could not sleep.

Next day, she booked an appointment with Dr Sonali. Shalini reached the doctor's office a little late. Dr. Sonali smiled at her and said calmly, " you had an another episode with Rohit." Shalini looked at her gravely and replied, " he wants to leave me." Dr Sonali asked unmoved, " what do you think will happen, if he leaves you?" Shalini becomes agitated. She answers, " I think I will cease to exist." Dr Sonali smiled, " why do you think your self worth is dependent on Rohit? Why is it so?" Shalini replies broken-hearted, " I feel I'm not worthy of love." Dr Sonali asks unfazed, " do you think Rohit resembles a part of yourself that you don't want to recognise in yourself?" Shalini looks at her therapist with surprise, " even Rohit said the same thing." Dr Sonali looked at her and continued," sometimes there are parts of our personality we do not recognise in ourselves instead project it on others. Though we feel we are extremely attached with that person in reality we are only attached to that aspect which we identify as ourselves. Shalini, there is no other. We keep falling in love with ourselves by projecting it on to others. Recognise that part of yourself that you project on Rohit."

Dr Sonali prescribed few more medications to Shalini to relieve her anxiety. Shalini reached home, took her medicine and go to bed. She wakes up, it is morning.

She feels fresh after a deep sleep. She goes to the kitchen to make herself a cup of tea. She brings her tea and sits at the study table. It's very quite, she is feeling very light. She doesn't remember when she felt so light. She thought about her conversation with Dr Sonali. Which part of her she identifies with Rohit. Shalini comes out of her reverie. Where is Rohit? Shalini feels a lightning pass through her spine. Where is her Rohit? And she suddenly thought, is he real? She rebuked herself on such silly thoughts. She looks around her house. He is not there. The thought hit her like a bolt, he has left her. She gets panic stricken, where can she find him. He doesn't have a phone, he is not on social media. The company he said he worked for has no record of him. Where will she find him? Shalini felt her whole world falling apart. She felt panic attacks.

It's one week since Rohit left . Shalini has not stepped out of her home. She is feeling acute panic attacks. She has not eaten for a week now. She is not responding to her calls. She has left her main door in case she is sleeping and Rohit comes and she doesn't hear the doorbell. She is feeling very weak almost as if she will faint. She doesn't remember if she is awake or sleeping. She hear footsteps, she sits up to look, she could see a silhouette of a person, she cries Rohit and everything goes blank.

Shalini opens her eyes. She saw a familiar face, it's Kavita. She looks around, she is in a hospital . The door opens and Dr Sonali comes in. She looks at Dr Sonali and smiles, " how are you, Shalini?" asks Dr Sonali. "

how did I get here?" asks Shalini . " Kavita called an ambulance and got you here", replies the doctor.

Kavita is Rohit's best friend since high school. After Rohit's parents death Kavita was the shoulder, he cried on. Rohit and Kavita shared everything with each other. Since last two years Rohit has become very secretive about his personal life. Rohit told her He was dating someone but he did not share the details. Rohit and Kavita work in the same office. Rohit has always been very punctual and a high performer. But, for one year He is taking too many offs from office. He doesn't like to go out with her. Earlier, they went for shopping together but gradually Rohit has stopped coming to their regular shopping trips. Even Rohit's appearance is changing too. He has lost a lot of weight. Rohit has always been very particular about his looks. But gradually He has become careless about it. Recently, He started looking dirty with dishevelled hair and crumbled clothes.

Since last two months Rohit became very irregular to office. Kavita knew Dr Sonali as she consulted her too. When Rohit did not come to office for two weeks and did not pick her phone. She went to meet Dr Sonali. Dr Sonali told her about Shalini. She decided to go to Rohit's house. The door was open she entered the apartment and went inside the bedroom suddenly Rohit sat up and cried Rohit and collapsed. She called Dr Sonali and on her advice she called an ambulance. She admitted Rohit in the hospital.

After admitting Rohit in the hospital Kavita goes back to Rohit's Apartment. She wanted to meet Shalini though he was not there when she went to Rohit's home. If nothing else she will find something about Shalini whom Rohit did not mention to her. Kavita opens the apartment and goes inside. She looks around but could not feel anyone living there other than Rohit. She opens the cupboard but only finds Rohit's clothes. She checked Rohit's desk to find any id proof Shalini but only finds Rohit's papers. She checks the bathroom but could not find any women toiletries. Confused she goes to meet Dr Sonali.

Dr Sonali sat silently at her office. She was thinking about Shalini's case. A knock on the door brought back Dr Sonali from her thoughts. It was Kavita. Dr Sonali signaled her to come inside and take a seat. "Who is Shalini?" asked Kavita. "Shalini is you Kavita", replied Dr Sonali. " Me!", asked Kavita surprised. " I want to ask a personal question. Has Rohit ever proposed you?"asked Dr Sonali. " yes he did but I refused bcoz Im in love with someone else", replied Kavita. Rohit is suffering from Schizophrenia. He has created Shalini in his mind to deal with his loss of losing you. He has not only created Shalini but has become Shalini who is searching for Rohit." " How do we make Rohit realise that Shalini is unreal", asks Kavita exasperated. Dr Sonali calmly replied, " First we have to make him realise that he is Rohit and then help him clear the confusion that Shalini is no other but you Kavita. Shalini is no other but a repressed part of Rohit. We have to build his confidence and help him realise self love."

A slight nudge from her publisher brought Shalini back to the present moment. She took a deep breath and replied," Rohit is a part of me. He is always with me not as a figment of my imagination but an important part of myself." Rohit smiled at the audience and stood up. He realised He is whole today; he doesn't need assurances by others about his own ability. He who is both Rohit and Shalini has realised love.

Unconditional Love

This is the moment I choose to live. In the hidden corners of my mind fear has marked it space. But I decide to choose this moment when I become one with my self. Surrendering in the comfort of my mind, in the joys of peace. I claim my happiness! Forgetting the litany of thoughts. The sharp prick of passing time. I steal this moment to be happy! To be beyond the walls of constraints, freeing my imagination to grow above the malign confinement of pain. I shoot into the sky, thunderous like lightning. I, Piya will find her home.

Piya came out from her reverie. The sun was melting in the horizon. The sky was permeated with hues of orange. Piya turned to look inside the room. Her room with sparse furniture, with a bed and a study table . Her eyes lingered on the dusty, large bookshelf standing beside her bed. A sombre expression enveloped her face. She browsed through the shelf when her gaze stopped lingered on a red book. Her heart swelled; it always does when she read her name on it. It was her first book. A labour of love! It was love that she wrote on those pages. Her love for Rahul… It was dedicated to him. Her two love of her life : Rahul and words. Now, both are bereft of her.

She walked to the book shelf and picked the red book. Caressing its bold red cover, Piya flipped the pages till she reached the first chapter. The dogeared page was titled 'Unsaid Promise'. Her eyes hovered on inked words studded on yellow paper-

'The music of words fills my heart of a dream, I dreamt long, long ago. The white clouds drifting in blue sky with promises of wonderland. I jump to reach them longingly to float in unabashed sky. I stare hard at them and wonder what they hide behind them. May be a fairyland or a sacred space where longings find their home or a faraway land of promises. May be a space where dreams come true and my desires find home. The clouds wander to unknown places into wild recesses of a distant land where I dream to go.

The wind sings along racing to touch the leaves in sweet caress. Meandering its way to reach the clouds as blobs of stark white move to cover the sun. The wind drew its breath to release the leaves clutching to the branch as the departing lovers. How mesmerizing it is to feel it cool caress in a hot summer day. Like water touching the parched lips. Dancing in its tune are the flowers in slow rhythmic fashion. Like dancers in a circle synchronizing their steps. How I wander where will it go from here? May be to a hill or forest whistling its story in silence.

I wait for sunset to spread the hues of orange and lavender. The horizon appears with a promise to meet a forgotten friend. I watch the sky from my window. How endless it is? Like a promise made long ago. That was never spoken but never forgotten!

Reminiscing the days gone by as if discovering a new path to an old lane. Now it feels unreal as if I read it in a book. Where its gone, a moment in which I rode on the clouds to wonderland. The leaf that left its branch to be swept away with the wind to an unknown, uncharted land. I'm left with the after taste! Longing again to find my way back to that moment. A moment felt like water which you can touch but cannot hold; liquid but palpable. My basket of memory is full of these ripe fruits that I want to savor again . Dig in my teeth in the viscous liquid of unlived moments. Reliving the crumbs of memory molding into the present time.

I long for those unfurled days just passing thru like clouds shifting away aimlessly and I just sit and let it goes by like the sky- unhurried, un-purposely. A silent street with row of houses existing in silo- mute but filled with unspoken tales . My mind wander heavy with images of my childhood. Like an era has ended . A lost dream somewhere folded in the crevices of my mind. Dust layered, partly forgotten like a dream of yesterday. Missing-in-parts but heavy with remnants.

The seasons pass like a fast- moving train and time is still! I walk back to the memory lane. Leading to the moments like scattered treasures. I dig in! I found gold as I drift to my old house. My home-as it still feels. Once a pillar of strength now lying under a debris. But in my memory its intact, forever. The clouds hovered above its roof, and garden. I remember, running through the rose beds. Touching its soft petals, inhaling its sweet scent. How I remember? its petals studded with dew on misty mornings and I just live its presence, encompassing its existence in my memory, forever etched. The clouds swept to far away lands. And I followed them. Leaving my safe space to an unknown land that I call home. Living a life that was born from moments I unlived.'

Pia stops reading abruptly. Her mouth parched and throat heavy. Tears swell from her eyes, unrestrained like a monsoon rain. She pushed down the lump in her throat. It's been a decade since Rahul left. Somehow it still feels like yesterday.

It was 2012, when Nirbhaya became the movement of brave women. Pia just completed her masters in psychology. She joined the non-violent protest at India Gate, Delhi. It was her first first time participation,her countenance demure, she walked with thousands to India Gate. Slightly awkward she sat in the second row. Suddenly, her eyes caught the eye of a man standing at the side. She looked at him searching in her mind if she knows him. He smiled at her and she remembered he was the guest lecturer in one of her psychology classes. She smiled back.

It was almost midnight when the protest closed. Pia was in two minds-whether to take a metro or a taxi to go back home. She was pondering the question when someone called her name. She turned to look and it was the guest lecturer. She was astounded that he knew her name.

' How do you know my name?' Pia asked perplexed

' I have a Eidetic memory. I never forget a name'. He said fondly

Pia beamed and said; ' What is your name?'

'Rahul'. He replied charmingly

The transition from strangers to friends was easy for Rahul and Pia. The rendezvous became frequent. Rahul was a rising psychotherapist and had a flourishing private practice. Pia found an anchor is

Rahul. A feeling of belongingness that she doesn't remember she ever felt before. Her Parents passed away when she was a kid. She was raised by her maternal uncle. Though her personal life was good but Pia always felt a melancholy she could not describe. Somehow, it vanished since she met Rahul. Like an inyeon- a connection that is born from fate; like an invisible bond that ties their souls forever.

Rahul Kapur, a well connected, rising psychotherapist with a long list of wealthy and famous clients. The list is long not only of clients but of series of unsuccessful relationships. Despite being a relationship counsellor he somehow could not apply his own advice. The long list of ex-girlfriends and some fiancé is due to Rahul's commitment phobia. However, Pia was different. Her presence filled him with happiness. Her embraces were a cool breeze on a summer evening. She quieted his restless spirit. It was unprecedented for Rahul to move in with his partner within three months of meeting her. But this happened with Pia. When he told Pia of his desire to share space with her, she was overjoyed. He visioned a fulfilling future with her. He finally felt like he was home in the arms of his beloved Pia.

Two years have passed since Pia and Rahul moved in together. Though everything was perfect but Pia was restless. Rahul was perfect! Her life is amazing but she wanted something more.

In these two years Pia has fulfilled her desire to become an author. She is a practicing psychotherapist now. The days pass by quickly but at night she can't sleep. Her thoughts wander about the uncertainty about future. Lately, she is feeling Rahul a little distant. May be it's the work. She knows what is gnawing her heart lately. The cause of her sleepless nights. Her desire to be a mother!

Becoming a mother was her secret desire since she was a teenager. In her imagination it is the most fulfilling feeling. Since her parent's demise she longed for her own family. That is when she decided she will get married and have her own kids. But when she discussed it with Rahul,he refused. She was hurt. She cried the whole night lying on the edge of the bed, away from Rahul . It was the first time she felt distant from him. The feeling of belonging passed away and she was left with loneliness.

Days went by but each passing day she seems to lose Rahul a little more. A year almost passed but she could feel silence between each other. Rahul is spending more time at his clinic. By the time he reached home, she already pretends to sleep. Her inner void is eating her alive. She knows that she has to reach out to Rahul.

It was January 2015 when Pia decided to finally face Rahul. She waited for him to come home Suddenly she hears the click of the lock and Rahul enters. Surprised to see her, Rahul smiled.

'Why are you still awake?' He asked

'I was waiting for you. We need to talk.' She replied awkwardly

'Let me change then we'll talk.' Rahul asked

' I hope its not about the same topic we discussed many times? You know my answer.' Rahul responded annoyingly

' But why?' Priya screamed

'I want a child! I can't go on living like this.' Priya grunts

' If you don't want children then what's purpose of this relationship?' asked Priya

'Then let's end it.' Rahul replied calmly then left the apartment.

Pia didn't stop him. The next day Rahul came to collect his belongings. Pia left for her clinic. When she returned in the evening, the apartment was half empty and there was no sign of Rahul's belonging. And just like that Rahul left.

Present Day

The hues of orange turned purple as the night befall and evening embraces the moon to become night. The doorbell rang, Pia skipped a heartbeat. She rushed to the door and open it. There she was the love of her life. A love that transforms everything and gave purpose to her life, Ananya.

After Rahul left Pia decided to adopt a baby girl. After waiting for one long year, her turn came. It was love at first sight . Ananya was round faced chubby baby with curious eyes. When Pia held her she knew she will sleep peacefully. Her small hands and tiny fingers touched Pia's hand she knew she was chosen to be her mother.

Now, a decade has passed since Rahul left. She is not in touch with him. The last she heard that he moved to US. Since then Pia has come a long way. Today. She is a one of the prominent Psychotherapist in the city. She has two clinics and long list of well connected clients.

Pia picks Ananya in her arms and a little closer than other days. Though she still misses Rahul but with Ananya she found herself. Before Ananya she didn't know her capacity to love unconditionally. Ananya completes her. With Ananya by her side she sleeps peacefully. That Void is filled with Joyous days and happy nights. She is never lonely. She found her calling in her daughter. A calling to love without expectation. She found her family. Pia laid the dinner on the table. As always she and Ananya eat their dinner watching Ananya's favourite cartoon. Today like always is the best day of Pia's life.s

About the Author

Uma Sharma

Uma is writer and editor. She writes on inclusivity, gender equality. She runs her own content agency. She resides in Gurugram. Her passion is reading and writing.

www.ingramcontent.com/pod-product-compliance
Lightning Source LLC
LaVergne TN
LVHW041639070526
838199LV00052B/3463